The Cowboy Next Door

PAUL SHIPTON

Illustrated by Sarah Nayler

Ballyroan Library
Orchardstown Ave
Rathfarnham, Dublin 14
Ph. 4941900

D0795423

OXFORD
UNIVERSITY PRESS

OXFORD
UNIVERSITY PRESS

Great Clarendon Street, Oxford OX2 6DP

Oxford University Press is a department of the University of Oxford.
It furthers the University's objective of excellence in research, scholarship,
and education by publishing worldwide in

Oxford   New York

Auckland   Cape Town   Dar es Salaam   Hong Kong   Karachi
Kuala Lumpur   Madrid   Melbourne   Mexico City   Nairobi
New Delhi   Shanghai   Taipei   Toronto

With offices in

Argentina   Austria   Brazil   Chile   Czech Republic   France   Greece
Guatemala   Hungary   Italy   Japan   Poland   Portugal   Singapore
South Korea   Switzerland   Thailand   Turkey   Ukraine   Vietnam

Oxford is a registered trade mark of Oxford University Press
in the UK and in certain other countries

Text © Paul Shipton 2007
Illustrations © Sarah Nayler 2007

The moral rights of the author have been asserted

Database right Oxford University Press (maker)

First published 2007

All rights reserved. No part of this publication may be reproduced,
stored in a retrieval system, or transmitted, in any form or by any means,
without the prior permission in writing of Oxford University Press,
or as expressly permitted by law, or under terms agreed with the appropriate
reprographics rights organization. Enquiries concerning reproduction
outside the scope of the above should be sent to the Rights Department,
Oxford University Press, at the address above

You must not circulate this book in any other binding or cover
and you must impose this same condition on any acquirer

British Library Cataloguing in Publication Data
Data available

ISBN: 978-0-19-846097-8

9 10

Available in packs

Stage 9 More A Pack of 6: ISBN 978-0-19-846092-3
Stage 9 Class Pack: ISBN 978-0-19-846099-2
Guided Reading Cards also available:
ISBN: 978-0-19-915230-8

Cover artwork by Sarah Nayler

Printed in China by Imago

Paper used in the production of this book is a natural,
recyclable product made from wood grown in sustainable forests.
The manufacturing process conforms to the environmental
regulations of the country of origin.

1
Perkins, the cowboy

Mrs Perkins lives next door to us.

One day she was going to the shops.

'Can you bring the washing in?' she asked Mr Perkins.

'Yes,' he said.

But Mr Perkins *didn't* bring the washing in.

Ten minutes later, we heard a yell from his house. 'YEE-HAH!'

'What's *that*?' asked my sister Jenny.

'There's a cowboy film on TV,' I said. 'Mr Perkins must be watching it.'

Soon Mr Perkins came out into his
garden. He had a cowboy hat on and a
hankie around his neck. He didn't have
cowboy boots, but he had wellies on.

'Hello, Mr Perkins,' I called.

Mr Perkins touched his hat with one finger. 'Howdy, Lucas,' he said to me. 'Howdy, little lady,' he said to Jenny.

My sister giggled.

Mr Perkins got the washing line and
tied a loop at one end. It was a lasso!

He began to swing it over his head.

'Yee-hah!' cried cowboy
Mr Perkins.

He threw the loop
towards a tree.

But it went past the tree.
It went over the fence.
It went over the bumper of a
passing truck.

Most cowboys would have let go, but
Mr Perkins was new to being a cowboy.
He *didn't* let go – and he ran all the
way into town.

Mrs Perkins wasn't happy when she saw the washing. She wasn't even happy that Mr Perkins was in the Sunday paper.

It said: 'Fastest Cowboy in the West'.

2
Perkins, the pirate

The next week, Mrs Perkins was going to the shops again.

'Can you dig the flowerbeds in the garden?' she asked Mr Perkins.

'Oh, yes,' he said.

But Mr Perkins *didn't* dig the flowerbeds.

He ran inside.

Chirp

'What's on TV, Lucas?' my sister
asked me.

'A film called "The Treasure of Skull
Island",' I said. 'It's about pirates.'

Soon Mr Perkins came out into his garden. He had an eye patch on and his hankie around his head.

He didn't have a parrot, but he had Mrs Perkins' budgie on his shoulder. It didn't look very happy.

Mr Perkins saw me and shouted,
'There's treasure on this island, lad!'
Jenny giggled.

Mr Perkins looked at a map and
walked around his garden.

At last, he stopped and began to dig
a big hole with his spade.

'Mrs Perkins won't like that,' I said
to Jenny.

But then we heard a CLANG! as the
spade hit something.

CLANG!

'Gold! I've found gold!' cried pirate Mr Perkins. He dug faster. But it wasn't gold. It was water – lots of it.

A big jet of water shot into the air.

Whoosh!

The budgie flew off with a squawk, but Mr Perkins was not so quick. He got very wet.

Mrs Perkins wasn't very happy when she saw her flowerbeds.

She wasn't even happy that Mr Perkins was in the Sunday paper *again*.

It said: 'Pirate Hits Water Pipe'.

3

Perkins, the King of the Jungle

The next week, Mrs Perkins was going to the shops again. She looked a bit worried.

'Can you do the dishes?' she asked Mr Perkins.

'Yes!' he said.

'*Just* the dishes?' said Mrs Perkins.

'Oh, yes!'

But Mr Perkins *didn't* do the dishes.
He went and sat down in front of
the TV.

I had a look to see what was on.
Oh no! There was a film called 'King
of the Jungle'. It was about a man who
lived with the animals in the jungle.

Jenny and I ran into the garden.
We didn't have long to wait.

Soon there was a loud yell.

'AAAAAA-OOOOOO-AAAAAAA-
OOOOOOOOO-AAAAAAAH!'

It was Mr Perkins
doing a King of
the Jungle cry.

Then he came into the garden.
He had on a pair of spotted swimming
trunks and a towel.
He didn't have
a knife, but he
had a spoon
hanging from
his belt.

'Me Perkins!'
he grunted.

Jenny and I grinned. Mr Perkins was looking at our paddling pool. The only thing in it was a blow-up toy crocodile.

Mr Perkins grabbed a branch of the apple tree and swung over the fence. The branch snapped and he fell.

'OW!'

He jumped up and ran towards
the pool.

'Me Perkins of the Jungle!' he shouted.

He jumped into the pool and began to
fight the crocodile. Water splashed
everywhere.

At last, Mr Perkins stood up and beat his chest with his fists.

'Perkins is King of the Jungle!' he yelled.

But suddenly there was a noise – HISSSSSSSS!

Mr Perkins froze.

He looked at the toy crocodile.
How could it make a noise?

Then the crocodile started
to move.

Jungle Mr Perkins' eyes were big.
How could it MOVE?

'Er...' said Mr Perkins.

He had just had an awful idea.
Perhaps it was ALIVE...

HISSSSSSSS!

'No,' thought Mr Perkins, as more air began to rush out of the crocodile.

It *was* a toy, and now it had a hole in it.

The crocodile zoomed off.

HISSSSSSS s s s

We watched it whizz all around
the paddling pool and over the fence
into the Perkins' garden.

Just then, there was a loud
yell from next door: 'OW!'

It was a burglar! He was coming out
of the Perkins' window with their TV!
The toy crocodile had hit him on the
head and knocked him down.

Mrs Perkins wasn't happy when she saw the police car outside her house. But she changed her mind when she heard all about the burglar. She was even happier when Mr Perkins was in the Sunday paper.

NEWS JUNGLE HERO CATCHES BURGLAR

The next week, Mrs Perkins was going to the shops.

Jenny and I were in the front garden.

'What's on TV?' my sister asked me.

I looked in the paper. 'It's a space film called "Robots from Planet X",' I said.

Mr Perkins had just put on the TV.
Mrs Perkins stopped at the gate.

She dropped her bags and ran back
to the house. 'Wait! I'm NOT going to
the shops today!' she shouted.

About the author

I grew up in Manchester, but
I have lived all over the place –
including America for ten
years. Now I live in Cambridge
with my wife and two
daughters.

Like many writers, I daydream a lot.
What would it be like to be a pirate?
A cowboy? Tarzan? In this story, Mr Perkins
just takes the daydreaming one step further.